TOY MOUNTAIN

First published 2021

EK Books
an imprint of Exisle Publishing Pty Ltd
PO Box 864, Chatswood, NSW 2057, Australia
226 High Street, Dunedin, 9016, New Zealand
www.ekbooks.org

A CiP record for this book is available from the National Library
of Australia.

ISBN 978-1-925820-96-6

Designed by Mark Thacker
Typeset in Minya Nouvelle 17 on 24pt
Printed in China

This book uses paper sourced under ISO 14001 guidelines from
well-managed forests and other controlled sources.

10 9 8 7 6 5 4 3 2 1

To OG – our planet needs you.
– S.G.

To Matilda Rosa.
– K.H.

TOY MOUNTAIN

STEF GEMMILL AND KATHARINE HALL

At the end of the rainbow, high up in the clouds, the Tiny Hands toy factory towered over the town.

Inside, busy hands made toys that rumbled, grumbled and plinked.

'They have so many new toys in the factory, Grandma,' said Sam. 'I only have old ones.'

'Your toys are special, Sam. Especially since I played with them at your age,' she said. 'And you're good at sharing them with baby Max.'

Sam sighed. He pushed the little train and watched Tooty chug off on wobbly wheels.

That night, Sam's mother came home with an announcement.

'Sam, the Tiny Hands Toy Company need a toy tester. Wouldn't that be fun?'

'Really?' gasped Sam. 'Please, can I be a toy tester?'

TOY TESTER WANTED!

'Done,' she said.

Ding-dong!

One big box arrived.

Sam *snipped* the string
and *ripped* the paper.
Out popped a silver
train that *clickety-
clacked* down the tracks.

Ding-dong!

Two big boxes arrived.

Sam *snipped* and *ripped*.

He pulled knobs that *popped* and flaps that *flopped*.

'Don't touch, Max. They're mine.'

That night, Sam dreamed of playing with his new toys over and over again.

Ding-dong!

'Good morning, Sam,' said the delivery man. Sam's eyes grew wide at the size of the box.

'Wake up, Max,' said Sam. 'Look how many toys I have.'

Sam pulled levers that pinged and hooted horns that honked. But as he tested his toys, they began to go *plonk*.

PLONK!

PLINK!

PLONK!

PLONK!

PLINK!

Ding-dong!

More trucks pulled up. More boxes piled up.

Toys tumbled from tables spilling out of the door.

Sam worked faster and faster.

Beep, bang, PLONK!

He tossed the toys high. Piling up, up, up
on top of a toy mountain.

All of a sudden, Sam stopped.

He found his drum had no *tap*,
his duck had no *quack* and his train
had no *toot*, just a *wheeze*.

'Poor Tooty,' he cried,
'and Ted is trapped too.'

Sam tugged Ted's arm.
But Ted was stuck.

'Max! Grandma! Please help
me save my old friends.'

HELP!
HELP!
HELP!
HELP!
HELP!
HELP!

Max pulled. Grandma pulled. Sam pulled.
The toy mountain teetered and tottered ...

Drums *tap-a-tapped!*

Ducky *quacked!*

Tooty *tooted!*

Teddy hugged.

And Sam smiled.

Sam's special
toys were home.